A MASSIVE CLEAN-UP

Wax figures of infamous villains have come to life and made a big mess at the Ninjago® Museum of History. Now the ninja must help the curator, Dr. Saunders, clean the place up.

THE TIME TWINS

The evil brothers known as the Time Twins want to gain control over time itself! But first, they need to find four secret blades. They are aided by an army of slithering snakes known as the Vermillion Warriors.

In each of the triangles below, choose the letters with the darkest background. Then put the letters together to decipher the twins' names. Write your answers in the empty frames.

THAT'S RIGHT! LET'S NOT WASTE ANY TIME!

THE FIRST TIME BLADE

Acronix touched Master Wu with the Forward Blade, which speeds up time. To find out what this dangerous weapon looks like, connect the dots from 1 to 32.

I HOPE YOU'LL ENJOY LIFE IN THE FAST LANE, OLD MAN!

WHERE IS MASTER WU?

After Acronix struck him with the Forward Blade, Wu became faster than lightning. He's too quick to see, but there are traces left behind. Look closely and show Lloyd the Wu who's identical to the one in the portrait.

I CAN'T BELIEVE WE HAVE TO CLEAN THIS PLACE UP. ISN'T THERE A BAD GUY OUT THERE WE COULD FIGHT INSTEAD?

DITTO!

OH! UNINVITED GUESTS!

WANT TO BET ON WHO CAN TAKE OUT THE MOST OF THEM? THE LOSER DOES CHORES!

CHALLENGE ACCEPTED! HERE GOES NUMBER ONE!

I'M UPPING THE ANTE!

BUT YOU'RE CHEATING!

NEXT! I FORESEE A NINJA IN BLUE CLEANING UP ALL BY HIMSELF!

THE TWINS' SECRET

The ninja have unmasked Krux! They can't believe that one of the Time Twins has been living in Ninjago City all this time . . . and he's someone they know and trust! Untangle the lines to reveal his false identity.

THE NEW MASTER

Lloyd wants to train with the other ninja. Put the Elemental Masters in order by filling the blanks with the right numbers. Make sure that no ninja repeats vertically or horizontally.

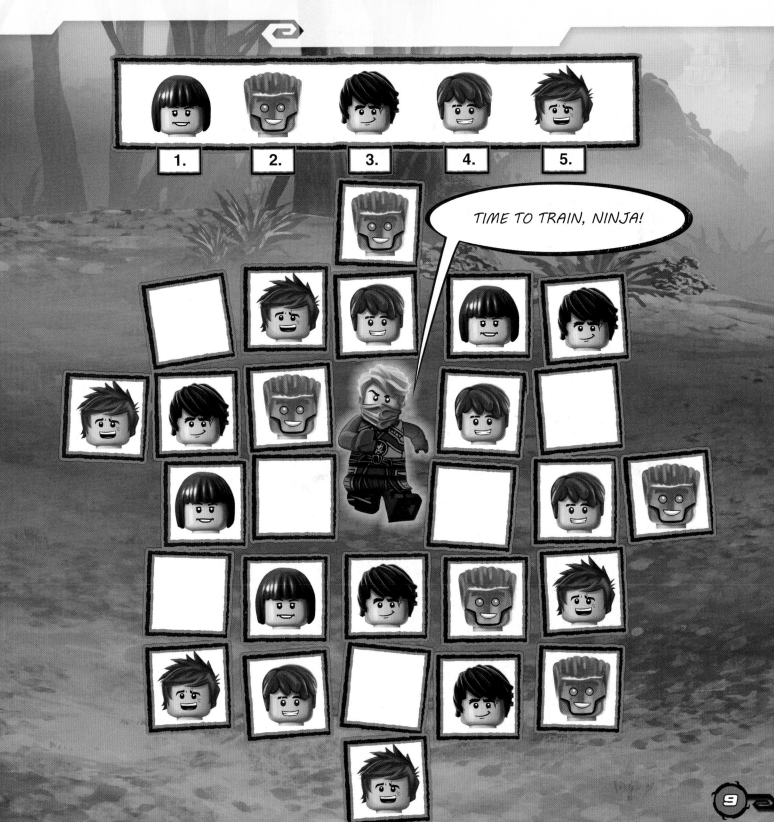

TIME TO TRAIN, NINJA!

TIMELESS CLASH

Nya and Kai are going head-to-head with the Time Twins in the Swamplands. This double duel is bound to end in an epic battle!

Look at the two pictures of this super sibling face-off, and circle ten differences between them.

STEEL VS. STEEL

BY JONATHAN EMPSON

Kai revved his bike as he raced through Ninjago City. The streets were eerily quiet after the first wave of Vermillion Warrior attacks.

Kai, Jay, Cole, and Nya had already faced their enemies on top of Borg Tower. They had even thrown a few off the roof, but the fall didn't seem to have much, um, of an impact. Red snakes slithered out of the shattered armor and reassembled themselves into new fighters.

And then the Vermillion Warriors had disappeared. But why? And where had they gone?

The ninja had jumped into their vehicles and raced off in different directions to find their foes. Their indestructible foes.

"Hmm," murmured Kai, "maybe sticking together would have been a better plan . . ."

Suddenly, he spotted two of the warriors down a side street. He twisted the throttle and charged toward them. They were dismantling the steel frame of a building that was under construction.

"Why did the builders have to use steel?" Kai sighed. "Haven't they ever heard of plastic bricks?"

Kai jumped off the bike and into the fray before the bike's wheels had even stopped turning — and before he'd counted how many foes he was up against.

Uh-oh.

There were two more Vermillion Warriors on the next floor up, busy unbolting beams. It didn't take advanced math to work out that made four enemies in all.

But there was no backing out now.

Kai soared up in a burst of Airjitzu, hurling fireballs at a beam one warrior was trying to remove. Instantly, the beam was welded into place.

Kai drew his sword as he landed on a higher beam. He slashed at the warrior, who was hopping around and blowing on his fingers, which he'd burned on the now searing-hot beam. The warrior crashed to the ground below and shattered. Snakes slithered out of the wrecked armor.

. . . and yep, the snakes slithered right back together again. The pieces wriggled toward one another, trying to reassemble.

"You guys give recycling a bad name," said Kai, leaping to the ground. He narrowly avoided the giant blade of another warrior on the upper level. His armor looked different — maybe he was a higher rank.

"Yield, human!" cried the new warrior, jumping down to confront Kai. "Resistance is futile."

"Yeah, whatever," said Kai. "People are always saying that to me. And you know what? It never is."

"What never is what?" said the warrior, looking confused.

"Futile. Resistance, remember?" said Kai. "Try to keep up."

Kai dodged the warrior's angry sword lunge. "So are you the guy in charge here, or what?"

"I am Commander Raggmunk!" said the warrior, circling. "And yes, I control these Vermillion Warriors with my thoughts!"

"Yeah? Too bad thinking isn't your specialty," said Kai. "Here's a tip: If you're going to dismantle a building, don't start with the ground floor. It makes the floors above it kind of unstable."

"Are you calling me stupid?" roared Raggmunk.

"Yup," said Kai.

Raggmunk charged, but his fury made him lose concentration. His blows were rushed and easy to fend off.

Now Kai attacked, forcing Raggmunk back.

Raggmunk touched a hand to his helmet to issue a thought-command to the two other warriors. "I am in need of assistance!"

The warriors dropped the beams they'd been carrying and closed in on Kai, surrounding him. Blow after blow came raining down on the ninja. There was no escape!

"Now you're not feeling so smart, are you?" cried Raggmunk. But suddenly, he flew backward, crashing into the beams of the building's ground floor.

"Cole!" cried Kai, recognizing an Earth Punch when he saw it. "And Jay!" he added, as a lightning bolt felled one of the other warriors.

Kai's two friends ran to his side. "How did you find me?" he asked.

"We just followed the noise and flames," said Jay. "Fighting quietly isn't exactly your specialty."

"That guy's lips move when he thinks," said Cole, nodding in Raggmunk's direction. "Did you notice that?"

As Jay and Cole tackled the other Vermillion Warrior, Kai rushed toward Raggmunk, who was staggering to his feet. But then Kai stopped abruptly. The whole building was starting to creak ominously!

"Guys!" Kai called out. "We need to get out of here — now!"

Jay and Cole didn't miss a beat. "*NINJA-GO!*" the three ninja cried in unison. They used Spinjitzu to get out of harm's way just as the entire building frame collapsed on top of Raggmunk and his warriors.

Cole, Jay, and Kai landed on a nearby rooftop and surveyed the wreckage.

"My bad," said Cole. "My direction was a little off with the whole Earth Punch thing."

"Well," said Kai. "They did kinda bring it down on themselves."

A muffled voice came from deep within the tangled metal. It was Raggmunk. "This isn't over! Do you hear?"

"Wow," said Jay. "I guess the guy's too dumb to know when he's beat."

"Yeah," said Kai. "You might say his determination is *steely*!"

SNAKE HUNT

The Time Twins want to use their combat armor against the ninja. Can you stop them? Draw three lines on the paths to block the snakes' path to the suit of armor.

A MASTER'S WISDOM

As the new Master, Lloyd needs to help the ninja train. He wrote notes on what each of his friends should focus on improving. Match Lloyd's notes to the Elemental Master they describe.

This ninja is too impatient.
Assignment: Wait patiently in line.

This ninja takes everything too seriously. Assignment: Tell one joke per day.

This ninja is way too relentless.
Assignment: Drink more green tea.

This ninja's mouth never stops.
Assignment: Take some quiet time.
Read a book.

This ninja has a lot of strength and a will to fight. Assignment: Take up gardening. It will be relaxing.

JAY

KAI

NYA

COLE

ZANE

THE A-MAZE-ING AMUSEMENT PARK

The ninja must reach the amusement park before the Vermillion Warriors steal all the metal. Can you help the ninja find the fastest way through the maze?

EGGY AMMUNITION

Watch out! Vermillion Warriors are shooting eggs at Zane from a catapult! Help the ninja knock as many eggs as they can out of the sky before they hit the ground and release more snakes. Draw three straight lines starting at the crosshair.

LIGHTNING CYCLE

To reduce the effects of the second Time Blade, Jay charges his motorbike, *Desert Lightning*, to hyperspeed. Circle the two pieces that can't be found in the main picture before the Master of Lightning catches up with Acronix.

RECON

QUITE AN ARMY THEY HAVE HERE.

JUST TELL ME HOW MANY THERE ARE!

AN HOUR LATER . . .

HEY, NYA! WE'RE DONE COUNTING. THERE'S 235 OF THEM.

HE'S WRONG. THERE'S 236!

235!

236!

QUIT BICKERING, OR YOU'LL GET CAUGHT!

OUR TOTAL NUMBER IS 235. AND WE HAVE YOU SURROUNDED!

HA! I TOLD YOU! THERE'S 235 OF THEM!!!

UH-HUH. 235 PROBLEMS EXACTLY!

NOW WE JUST NEED TO TAKE CARE OF A FEW PROBLEMS . . .

SPOT THE SYMBOLS

The Vermillion Warriors have stolen two Time Blades from the Temple of Airjitzu. But which one stole the precious items? Study the picture and find the armor that has symbols identical to the ones shown in the box at the bottom of the next page.

QUICK QUIZ

The ninja have to work fast to defeat the Time Twins. How quickly can you answer the questions in this quiz?

1. What's the name of the Ninjago City museum curator?
a. Dareth S. Anders
b. Dr. Saunders
c. Dr. Smile

2. What made Master Wu start aging rapidly?
a. Forward Blade
b. Boots of Speed
c. Elixir of Haste

3. The Time Twins are actually called:
a. Krux and Adonis
b. Knox and Acronix
c. Krux and Acronix

4. What animals are Vermillion armor animated by?
   a. Spiders
   b. Lizards
   c. Snakes

5. Which ninja battled the Time Twins in the Swamplands?
   a. Lloyd and Zane
   b. Nya and Kai
   c. Cole and Jay

6. What special power does Jay's Lightning Cycle have?
   a. Shuriken launcher
   b. Lightning strikes
   c. Hyperspeed

7. What power does the second Time Blade have?
   a. Time slows down
   b. Time stops
   c. Time goes backward

ANSWERS

Pg. 1
A MASSIVE CLEAN-UP

Pgs. 2-3
THE TIME TWINS

ACRONIX

KRUX

Pg. 8
THE TWINS' SECRET

2.

Pg. 4
THE FIRST TIME BLADE

Pg. 5
WHERE IS MASTER WU?

Pg. 9
THE NEW MASTER

Pgs. 10-11
TIMELESS CLASH

Pg. 17
SNAKE HUNT

Pgs. 18-19
A MASTER'S WISDOM

1 - KAI
2 - ZANE
3 - NYA
4 - JAY
5 - COLE

Pgs. 20-21
THE A-MAZE-ING AMUSEMENT PARK

Pgs. 22-23
EGGY AMMUNITION

Pg. 24
LIGHTNING CYCLE

Pgs. 26-27
SPOT THE SYMBOLS

Pgs. 28-29
QUICK QUIZ

1 - b, 2 - a, 3 - c, 4 - c,
5 - b, 6 - c, 7 - a.

HOW TO BUILD
A VERMILLION WARRIOR

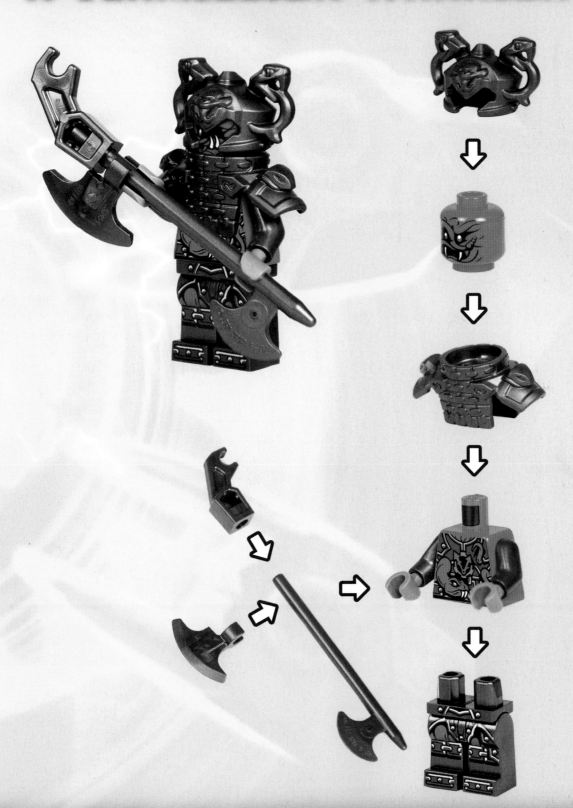